7-18   9-11   10/14   9/23
1-17   6-11   6/14   12/21
100   96   102   123
        1

COME AND HAVE FUN

by EDITH THACHER HURD

Pictures by Clement Hurd

An *EARLY* I CAN READ Book®

Harper & Row, Publishers

COME AND
HAVE FUN

"Mouse, mouse,

Come out of your house.

Come out of your house,"

said the cat to the mouse.

"Who me?" said the mouse.

"Come out of my house?"

"Yes, yes," said the cat.

"Come out of your house.

Come and have fun.

Come sit in the sun."

"Who me?" said the mouse.

"Sit in the sun?"

"Yes, yes," said the cat.

"That would be fun."

"No, no," said the mouse.

"That would not be fun.

You are a cat.

I am a mouse.

A cat and a mouse

do not have fun."

"Come, come," said the cat.

"Come and play ball.

Come and have fun."

"No, no," said the mouse

in his little mouse house.

The mouse would not play,

so the cat went away.

The mouse looked out of

his little mouse house.

"Where is the cat?"

said the mouse.

"He will run after me

if I come out of

my little mouse house."

The cat sat and sat.

The mouse sat and sat.

The mouse looked and looked.

He did not see the cat.

"I will come out," said the mouse.

"The cat will not see me

come out of my house."

But the cat did see.

The cat did see the mouse

come out of his house.

Away went the mouse.

Away went the cat.

"Oh, oh," said the mouse

as he ran and he ran.

"I must run fast,

as fast as I can."

Where? Where?

Where is the mouse?

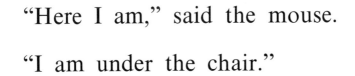

"Here I am," said the mouse.

"I am under the chair."

Away went the cat.

Away went the mouse.

He ran and ran.

He ran just as fast as

a little mouse can.

Up

down

in and out.

23

Where? Where?

Where is the mouse?

"Here I am," said the mouse.

"In my little mouse house."

"Come in," said the mouse.

"Come into my house."

The cat tried and tried.

He pushed and he pushed.

But only his whiskers

went into the house.

He pushed and he pushed.

But only his tail

went into the house.

"Oh, dear," said the mouse.
"I am sorry you cannot
come into my house.
We could have tea."

"Come out," said the cat.

"Come out and have tea."

28

"Oh, no," said the mouse

in his safe little house.

"I know what cats like best

for their tea!"

So the mouse in his house

drank his little mouse tea.

The cat sat outside

as sad as could be.

"Come, come," said the cat.

"Come play with me."

"Not I," said the mouse.

Then he wrote with his tail.

He put the mouse sign

on a little mouse nail: